Stacy Gregg (Ngāti Mahuta/Ngāti Pukeko) is the author of Pony Club Secrets, the inspiration for the major TV series MYSTIC. www.stacygregg.co.uk

Books by Stacy Gregg

The Spellbound Ponies Series

MAGIC AND MISCHIEF
SUGAR AND SPICE
WISHES AND WEDDINGS
FORTUNE AND COOKIES

The Pony Club Secrets series

MYSTIC AND THE MIDNIGHT RIDE
BLAZE AND THE DARK RIDER
DESTINY AND THE WILD HORSES
STARDUST AND THE DAREDEVIL PONIES
COMET AND THE CHAMPION'S CUP
STORM AND THE SILVER BRIDLE
FORTUNE AND THE GOLDEN TROPHY
VICTORY AND THE ALL-STARS ACADEMY
FLAME AND THE REBEL RIDERS
ANGEL AND THE FLYING STALLIONS
LIBERTY AND THE DREAM RIDE
NIGHTSTORM AND THE GRAND SLAM
ISSIE AND THE CHRISTMAS PONY

Pony Club Rival series

THE AUDITIONS
SHOWJUMPERS
RIDING STAR
THE PRIZE

For older readers

THE PRINCESS AND THE FOAL
THE ISLAND OF LOST HORSES
THE GIRL WHO RODE THE WIND
THE DIAMOND HORSE
THE THUNDERBOLT PONY
THE FIRE STALLION
PRINCE OF PONIES
THE FOREVER HORSE

Spellbound Ponies

Wishes and Weddings

STACY GREGG

HarperCollins *Children's Books*

First published in Great Britain by
HarperCollins *Children's Books* in 2021
HarperCollins *Children's Books* is a division of HarperCollins*Publishers* Ltd
HarperCollins Publishers
1 London Bridge Street
London SE1 9GF

www.harpercollins.co.uk

HarperCollins*Publishers*
1st Floor, Watermarque Building, Ringsend Road
Dublin 4, Ireland

1

ISBN 978-0-00-840293-8

Typeset in Cambria Regular 12/24
Printed and bound in the UK using 100% renewable electricity
at CPI Group (UK) Ltd

MIX
Paper from
responsible sources
FSC™ C007454

For Hilda and Buddy

Chapter One

Summoning a new pony was always a magical moment at Spellbound Stables. Olivia had woken early that morning, ready to meet her friend, Eliza, at the yard. Except . . .

'Muuuummm!' Olivia wailed. 'I can't find my jodhpurs! Where are they?'

Mrs Campbell stuck her head round the corner of the door. 'Livvy! How on earth do you expect to find anything in here? Clean your room! I've been asking you to do it for weeks.'

'I'm going to do it later!' Olivia insisted. 'But I need to get to the stables first!'

'What could possibly be going on at an old abandoned stables that suddenly requires such immediate attention?' Mrs Campbell snapped. 'Really, Olivia! Stop endlessly wiggling out of it – stay at home and CLEAN. YOUR. ROOM!'

Mrs Campbell left Olivia to it, shutting the bedroom door firmly behind her.

'She's such a grump!' Olivia muttered and then began flitting madly about the room, grabbing grubby laundry off the floor. She tried to shove the dirty clothes under her bed – only to find that it was crammed tight under there already!

'Rats! No room!' Olivia lugged the pile over to the wardrobe but when she opened the doors an avalanche of unwashed socks and gym gear tumbled out.

Olivia groaned. Now the mess looked even worse than before! And the clock on the wall had just struck nine. Olivia looked around at the utter chaos and knew she had no choice. There was no way she'd get the room clean in time; the only way out without her mum seeing was via the window.

A moment later, she clambered out and dropped down to the garden path, slinking alongside the house. In the kitchen she could hear her mum rattling pans and she scuttled like a beetle all the way to the garden gate and then out and along behind the hedge until she reached the lane.

Running to the end of her cul-de-sac, she turned down a pebbled lane, and there at the end were the grand old ivy-covered stone buildings of Pemberley Stables.

The stables were very ancient and the front doors had been locked tight, forbidding entry to all who tried to get in. For Olivia, though, they slid apart easily upon her touch, and she slipped hastily inside.

'Eliza?' Olivia hissed into the gloom. 'It's me! Where are you . . .?'

At the sound of Olivia's voice there was an urgent stamp of hooves on straw and two ponies appeared,

thrusting their magnificent heads over the doors of
the first two looseboxes.

Olivia felt her heart skip at the sight of them.
'Darling Bess!' she said, hugging the first pony,
a beautiful jet-black mare, who nickered with
joy as they embraced. 'And my handsome Prince!'

Olivia turned to stroke the dapple-grey gelding in the next stall as he shook his mane and snorted, his deep liquid-brown eyes trained on the dark-haired girl.

'Hello, my lovelies,' Olivia cooed. 'Have you seen Eliza anywhere?'

'I'm here!' said Eliza.

'Yikes!' Olivia shrieked. From out of nowhere a girl had appeared in the dark corridor behind her. She wore an antique nightgown, pale white against her ivory skin. She had bright green eyes and long curly red hair piled up in a messy bun. She looked about the same age as Olivia, which was nine. But Eliza was quite a bit older than that. Two hundred and nine, in fact!

'How many times have I asked you not to do that?' Olivia said.

Eliza giggled. 'Sorry – I didn't mean to spook you.'

Olivia smiled. 'It's okay. I guess it's to be expected when you're best friends with a ghost.'

'You're awfully late!' Eliza pointed out. 'I was getting worried you weren't going to come today.'

'Sorry! It was Mum's fault! But I'm here now. Are you ready to go on another adventure?'

Olivia definitely was. After all, it was up to them to break the spell cast over the stables two hundred years ago by the Pemberley Witch. It was this spell that had once cursed Bess and Prince to each be naughty in their own way – Bad Bess the highway horse had been a thief and Prince had been greedy.

For the other ponies the spell remained binding until the girls could set them free.

The words of the curse were written in the stone

15

of the stable walls beneath the overgrown ivy by the front door:

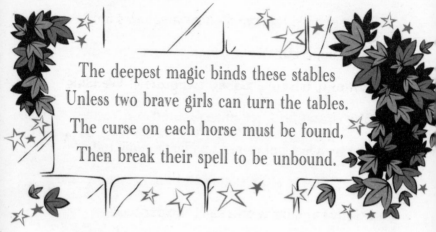

The deepest magic binds these stables
Unless two brave girls can turn the tables.
The curse on each horse must be found,
Then break their spell to be unbound.

'Umm, about the summoning, Livvy . . . I have something to tell you . . .' Eliza said nervously.

'What is it? Is there a . . .?' Olivia began, but before she could say anything more she was interrupted by some very strange sounds coming from behind the third door along the corridor.

'Oh, darling prince! Mwah-mwah! Ooooh, nuptials is near!'

'What on earth was that?' asked Olivia.

'Ah, see, that's what I need to tell you.' Eliza shifted uncomfortably from foot to foot. 'Because, you know, you were running late, and I was only fooling around but—'

'Whinny, whinny, babes! Ding-dong! Wedding bells!'

'Oh my sweet potatoes!' said Olivia. 'What is that?'

'That,' said Eliza with a sigh, 'is Sparkle.'

'Sparkle?' Olivia was baffled now. 'What's a Sparkle?'

'Sparkle is our next Spellbound pony,' Eliza said. 'While I was waiting for you to arrive I saw her name materialise on the door and I must have spoken it out loud as I stumbled over the threshold and triggered the summoning by mistake, and now she's in already in there . . . and, well, she's not at all what I expected!'

'What do you mean?' Olivia said.

'You'll see,' Eliza said. 'But be prepared! That witch's curse has done its worst and Sparkle is the most Spellbound pony we've encountered yet. I don't know if we can fix this one.'

'There's only one way to find out,' Olivia replied.

Eliza grinned. 'Are you ready to step inside the stall and meet our newest Spellbound pony?'

Chapter Two

Olivia blinked in the darkness. 'Ooh, I'm blind as a bat! Where are the lights?' She flicked on the switch and gasped. 'Eliza? Where on earth is the pony? She's gone!'

The stall was completely empty . . . except for a giant heap of muck that had been dumped right in the middle of the room on top of the straw.

Eliza groaned. 'She's not gone at all. You're

looking straight at her!'

And then Olivia saw that the mud heap was wobbling a little. Not just wobbling, but kind of jiggling and then . . . it spoke!

'Hello, babes!' the mud heap trilled.

'Eek!' Olivia shrieked. 'The mud just spoke to me!'

The mud heap began jiggling even harder at this and a cloud of dust rose up as it gave a tinkling laugh.

'Oh, babes! Me a mud 'eap? You must be joking! Whatever are you on about?' The mud heap moved closer to Olivia and out of the gloom of the stall and now she could see that it had legs! And eyes, and a muzzle!

'Livvy,' said Eliza with a sigh, 'this is Sparkle.'

'You mean underneath all that mud is a pony?' Olivia gasped.

'She never used to be like this,' Eliza said. 'I can remember her well.'

Olivia nodded. Of course Eliza would know
what the pony had been like. They had once
been her very own ponies – until the day she'd
had a fateful fall from her beloved pony, Chessie.
Heartbroken, her mother, Lady Luella, called upon
the Pemberley Witch to put a curse on the ponies to
punish them and they had been trapped in time.

'When Sparkle was a real-life pony she was
brilliant white, well groomed and with a silken mane
and a lustrous tail that were the envy of all,' Eliza
went on.

'Poor Sparkle!' Olivia said. 'The Pemberley Witch
has turned her into a mud-caked mess!'

'Oooh, babes, don't worry.' Sparkle shook her
dusty mane. 'You took Sparkle by surprise is all.
Give me a quick minute to fix myself up a bit . . .'

The mud heap shambled off to the other side
of the stall and dug about in the hay, and when she

returned there was a tiara stuck sideways in her forelock and she had drawn all over her grubby muzzle with bright pink lipstick.

'There!' Sparkle said. 'Sparkle's all gorgey-porgey now! What do you reckon?'

'Uhhh, much better?' Olivia still couldn't quite believe her eyes.

'Come in, come in, and make yourself comfy!' Sparkle swished the muddy thicket that passed for her tail and gestured for Olivia and Eliza to join her.

'Sit down! Sit down!' Sparkle beckoned, and Olivia noticed now that the stall was more like a teenager's bedroom than a stable. There was a bed with a duvet with hearts and crowns all over it and the walls were smothered in pictures torn from magazines.

'This looks exactly like my sister Ella's bedroom!' Olivia said.

The posters on the walls all seemed to be of the same blond-haired boy. In the photos he was often doing very dashing things like sailing a ship or sword fighting or horse riding.

'Who's that boy?' she asked.

Sparkle chortled. 'Livvy, Livvy, Livvy! You've been living under a rock, babes! You must know Prince Patrick!'

'I'm afraid I don't . . .' Olivia replied. 'But you seem to like him a lot!'

'Oh, everyone loves Patrick,' Eliza agreed. 'He's very popular. Handsome, charming – you know, the usual stuff.'

'He's a dashing prince!' Sparkle confirmed. 'And now he's getting married!'

'So there's going to be a royal wedding,' Eliza said. 'And who is the bride?'

'Why the princess-to-be is Lady Petronella!' Sparkle cried. 'It's been in all the papers! They're completely over the moon in love! It's going to be the most amazey-mazey wedding dazey! I simply cannot wait! I am all lovey-la-la! Ding-dong! Wedding bells! Huzzah!'

Sparkle began rushing around her stall now, sticking her muzzle up against the posters and smothering the prince with sloppy pink-lipstick kisses and pony slobber. 'Mwah! Mwah!'

'Sparkle,' Eliza said, 'maybe you should calm down a bit?'

'He gave her a diamond ring and they've announced the date!' Sparkle trilled. 'Ding-dong! Hear those wedding bells ring!'

Olivia was confused. 'I'm sure it's going to be very lovely for both of them, but what does this wedding have to do with you, Sparkle?'

'Duh! You are joking, right?' Sparkle chortled. 'It has *everything* to do with Sparkle! Don't you see, babes? I'm the pony that Lady Petronella is going to ride in the royal wedding procession!'

'You?' Olivia boggled.

'Me!' Sparkle said proudly. 'Sparkle's going to be the star of the whole thing! All the other ponies are going to be well jel when they see me in the procession!'

Olivia looked long and hard at the mud heap on four legs in front of her. 'Hmmmm, really Sparkle? The princess-to-be chose you?'

'Well, not yet, babes!' Sparkle said. 'But she will! I've filled in the application form. And now Lady Petronella and her beloved Prince Patrick are on their way here to inspect me!'

'What?!' Olivia squeaked. 'Please tell me you're joking, Sparkle!'

'Sparkle never jokes, babes,' the pony trilled. 'Their Royal Highnesses are going to be here any minute now!'

'That's it!' Olivia said. 'Eliza! I think I know what we need to do to break the witch's spell.

Sparkle must have been cursed to be messy. We must convince her to tidy up her act so that Lady Petronella chooses her to be in the royal wedding procession and the spell will be broken.'

'Yes,' Eliza agreed. 'Good idea, Livvy. Except . . .'

'What?'

'Sparkle is a mud heap,' Eliza said.

There was the blare of trumpets outside.

'And the princess-to-be is already here!'

Chapter Three

From outside the stall was the sound of trumpets and a spooky enchanted mist began to seep in.

Olivia felt her heart hammering. 'Oh no! Quick! Sparkle, we have to get you cleaned up!'

'There's no time!' Eliza said.

Olivia grabbed Sparkle by the halter. 'We have to at least try.'

'Steady on, babes!' Sparkle trilled. 'There's no need to fuss. I'll slap on some lippy and a spritz of perfume and that'll do the trick!'

'No, Sparkle!' Olivia grunted as she pulled at the pony's halter. 'You need a proper clean-up with soap and water!'

At these words Sparkle began to tremble. 'You mean a . . . a . . . bath?'

'That's right!' Olivia sang. 'It's bath day, Sparkle! Happy bath day! Happy bath day to you!'

'Not likely, babes!' Sparkle gave a swish of her tail. 'Sparkle's on the trot!'

And suddenly Sparkle wasn't there any more. She had magically slipped out of her halter and bolted clean through the wall of her stall!

'Ummm, Livvy?' Eliza said.

'What?' Olivia replied.

'She's gone.'

31

Olivia sighed. 'I can see that! I'd forgotten that the Spellbound ponies had the power to turn all spooky and *whoosh* through walls like that.'

'She really didn't want to have that bath, did she?'

'It's the witch's spell,' Olivia said. 'Sparkle doesn't realise she's enchanted. We'll have to find her and convince her to let us clean her before—'

Tan-ta-ta-ran-tan-ta-raaaaah!

'Too late,' Eliza said. 'Look!'

Through the stable doors came a marching band of royal trumpeters, followed by footmen in smart uniforms unfurling a red carpet in front of them across the stable floor.

The head footman stepped forward and cleared his throat. 'May I have your attention please? Announcing His Royal Highness Prince Patrick and his princess-to-be Lady Petronella!'

The trumpets blarted again and, amid a silvery swirl of enchanted mist, Prince Patrick, dashing in his red and gold-braided uniform, strode down the carpet with his bride-to-be at his side.

'Oooh,' Eliza said, sighing. 'The prince really is awfully handsome, isn't he? I can see why Sparkle has such a crush.'

'And Sparkle was right about Lady Petronella too,' Olivia said. 'She's very beautiful.'

Lady Petronella had long golden hair that fell in glossy waves past her shoulders and she was dressed in a turquoise-blue gown that matched her eyes. She clutched Prince Patrick fiercely by the arm as she gazed up at him adoringly.

'Patrick-wattrick,' she cooed. 'How sweet of you to come with me and look at ponies.'

'Well, you did insist, my lovely princess-to-be!' Patrick laughed nervously and Olivia couldn't help noticing that he managed to squirm out from her vice-like grip. 'You said you wanted every tiny, tiny detail of our wedding day to be absolutely right, and that you need the perfect pony for you to ride. Well, here we are, and I'm sure you'll be happy – Pemberley Stables has the very best ponies in the land.'

Lady Petronella turned her laser gaze from the prince and locked her blue eyes on to Olivia and Eliza. Her charming smile instantly vanished and her face became sullen and frowny.

'Well? Where's this wedding pony then?' she snarled. 'I haven't got all day! I've got such a long to-do list! There's the dress fitting after this – the dim-witted seamstress still can't get my sleeves puffy enough! And then there's the wedding flowers for the bouquet, which are a complete disaster! Not enough roses and lilies! And the wedding cake tastes of too much fruit! Oh, it's all wrong, wrong, wrong!'

'Hmmm, yes, weddings can be so tricky, can't they?' Eliza spoke carefully. 'And I do so hate to add to your problems, Your Almost Highness, but . . .'

Petronella's eyes narrowed. 'But what? Don't tell me there's something wrong with my pony?'

'No!' Olivia leaped forward. 'No. Nothing wrong at all, Lady Petronella. Your pony, Sparkle, is utterly fabulous. It's just that we were thinking it would be best if you came back another time to see her.'

'But I'm here now!' Petronella said. 'Where is she? I want her!'

'Ahhh yes,' Eliza said. 'Of course you do. And we'd bring her out too except—'

'Except . . .' Olivia added hastily, 'except you're not wearing your wedding dress!'

Petronella glared at them both. 'You two seem like quite a funny pair. You're even dressed like court jesters!'

Olivia looked at Eliza, who was wearing the clothes she had lent her, and at her own stripey top and dungarees. 'Are we?'

'You most certainly are,' said Lady Petronella, sniffing. 'Now tell me! Why should I be dressed in my wedding dress to look at a pony?'

'Yes, Livvy,' Eliza said. 'Please explain that to all of us, will you?'

Olivia gulped hard. She could feel her heart racing. 'Because, Lady Petronella, surely you know it's customary for royal brides-to-be to meet their pony in the bridal gown so that we can make sure that the dress matches the pony in exactly the same shade of white?'

'Ooooh yes!' Eliza hurried to agree. 'To check the colour, of course! And also the length.'

Petronella frowned. 'The length?'

'Uh-huh.' Olivia jumped back in. 'The dress must drape perfectly over the pony once you're on board. I mean, you wouldn't want the dress to be too long and drag on the ground, would you?'

'No,' Petronella admitted. 'No, I suppose I wouldn't want that. It would get grubby if it dragged, and I do so dislike things that are grubby.'

'Exactly!' Olivia said. 'So, since you don't have the dress with you this time, why don't we reschedule? Perhaps the same time tomorrow? You bring the dress and we'll have Sparkle all sorted and waiting for you.'

Petronella frowned. 'Are you fooling with me, little jester? I hope this isn't a joke you're playing on me because I don't like jokes one bit!'

'Oh no,' Olivia said. 'It's not a joke.'

'We are definitely not funny,' Eliza added.

'Good!' Petronella said. 'Because the last time someone played a joke on me, I took them to the castle and had them thrown in the dungeons! Didn't I, Patrick?'

'Er, yes, darling, you did,' Prince Patrick agreed.

'You don't want to go in the dungeons, do you?' Petronella said to the girls, the diamonds on her tiara twinkling like mad. 'Because I can put you there with a snap of my fingers. Is that what you want?'

Olivia gulped. 'Not really.'

Lady Petronella gave a tinkling laugh. 'Didn't think so!' she trilled. And then she spun round and clicked her fingers. 'Come on, Princey Pat. Let's go and check on that dressmaker. I want see if my dress sleeves are puffy enough yet!'

Hastily the trumpeters picked up their tune again and the footmen raced nervously up the red carpet, dropping rose petals ahead of Lady Petronella as she stomped back through the stables and out of the door.

The prince watched her go and held back, dawdling for a moment.

'She's in a bit of a mood today,' he said with a sigh. 'Mind you, she's in a bit of a mood most days.'

'Have you been engaged for long?' Olivia asked him.

'Only a couple of weeks,' Patrick admitted. 'My parents – the king and queen – said it was time for a royal wedding, and Lady Petronella is the perfect almost-princess to be my bride.'

'She certainly does seem to have some . . . unique qualities!' Eliza tried to be positive. 'And I suppose you both have lots in common?'

'Not really,' Prince Patrick said. 'She mostly likes shouting and putting people in the dungeons and I like sword fighting with my friends and sailing boats and riding horses.'

'Oh, I love all those things too!' Eliza said. 'Do you know I once sailed all the way to Spain? And I can outride almost any boy and I'm particularly good at sword fighting.'

'Really?' Prince Patrick smiled at her. 'How nice to meet a girl who likes the things that I like too! We should get together some time and go riding and have a sword fight and a picnic afterwards!'

'A picnic! That would be lovely,' Eliza said. 'How about—'

'Patrick!'

Lady Petronella was standing in the doorway with a face like thunder.

'Don't make me come back in there,' she growled, 'or you'll be in the dungeons too!'

Prince Patrick gulped. 'Coming straight away, my beloved!'

And with a regal wave farewell he bolted up the red carpet and out of the door and in a swirl of magic mist he was gone.

Chapter Four

Olivia woke up in a surprisingly sunny mood despite the setbacks of the day before. At least they'd managed to convince Lady Petronella to give Sparkle a second visit and Olivia felt positive that once they sat Sparkle down and explained to the poor Spellbound pony that the witch's spell was making her so very messy, she would certainly agree to have a bath.

'It's perfect pony-washing weather!' Olivia hummed to herself as she banged along the lane with her water buckets filled with sponges and soap. She slid open the front door of the stables and stepped into the gloomy corridor. 'Eliza? Are you here yet?'

In the darkness Eliza suddenly appeared beside her in a poof.

'Eek!' Olivia jumped in fright.

'Sorry!' Eliza giggled. She looked at the wash-up stuff Olivia had brought with her. 'Gosh, you look ready for business!'

'It's Mum's car-cleaning kit,' Olivia said. 'I thought we could use it to scrub up Sparkle.'

'Perhaps let's keep the buckets hidden behind our backs at first so as not to scare her?' Eliza cautioned. 'After all, we don't want her to disappear on us again!'

'Don't worry,' Olivia said, 'I'm sure when we explain the witch's spell then Sparkle will be willing

44

to help us and . . . Hey! What's that music?'

'Oh!' Eliza said. 'You can hear it too? I thought it was just me! I often have a tune in my head.'

'A tune?' Olivia boggled. 'Eliza, it's more than a tune! It's like there's a disco in there!'

It was true; the drum 'n' bass rhythm was pumping with a thumping beat and there were high-pitched whistles and noisy shrieks.

Olivia opened the stall door and immediately a thick blanket of spooky mist rolled out and completely engulfed the entire corridor.

'Oh no!' Eliza cried. 'Enchanted mist!'

Olivia coughed as a gust of the mist went up her nose. 'Gah! Eliza, I don't think it is enchanted mist. I've smelled this before at the school disco. I think it's coming from a smoke machine!'

Sure enough, just at that moment, the mist cleared a little and Olivia and Eliza could see inside Sparkle's stall where there was indeed a machine pumping out smoke. A glittering mirror ball was strung from the ceiling and a flashing whirl of brilliant coloured strobe lights was bouncing off the walls.

Olivia was stunned. 'It's exactly like a school disco!'

And standing in the middle of the dance floor, all dressed in a rainbow-coloured disco suit that stretched as tight as a drum across his rotund tum, was Horace the Hunt Master.

'Why, it's the girls!' Horace boomed over the disco beats.

'Horace?' Olivia couldn't believe it. The hunt master had been a friend of Lady Luella's and usually appeared when he wanted to keep the ponies trapped by their spell but he normally wore a red huntsman jacket and jodhpurs, not a disco dancer's leotard.

'It's definitely him,' Eliza confirmed. 'Look! You can tell by the way his head is boing-boinging in time to the music!'

Horace the Hunt Master had broken his neck in that famous, fateful hunting accident two hundred years ago and had never forgiven Eliza for what happened that day. As revenge he was determined to do whatever he could to keep the ponies spellbound forever. Unfortunately for the girls he had ways of keeping the poor gullible ponies in his thrall.

'Horace!' Olivia had to shout to be heard over the music. 'Where's Sparkle? What have you done with her?'

The hunt master wiggled his chubby fingers. 'Hands are for helping and I've been busy giving Sparkle the most magical makeover. Sparkle? Come on out, my dancing queen!' he called into the smoke.

Through the mist a monstrous sticky heap shambled into the glare of the disco lights, all shiny and globby, covered in rainbow glitter.

'Hey, babes!' the glitter glob trilled. 'Sparkle's a disco diva!'

'Sparkle! Ewwww!' Olivia grimaced. 'You're still covered in mucky wet mud and now you've added glitter!'

Horace chortled. 'Sparkle didn't want to wash, did you, sweets? So we just covered the mud in glue and then I launched glitter bombs at her!'

'The bombs did tickle a bit when they hit,' Sparkle burbled, 'but it was worth it. Sparkle's gorgey-porgey now!'

'I bedazzled her,' Horace confirmed.

'You mean you bewitched her!' Olivia snapped back at him. 'You want her to fail and stay messy forever.'

Horace giggled with glee. 'Of course I do!'

'Sparkle,' Olivia groaned, 'you're still messy

and dirty. You'll never get chosen for the royal wedding procession looking like this! You have to let us wash you and start again before it's too late!'

'It's already too late.' A cut-glass voice stabbed through the stables and the music instantly died.

Lady Petronella was standing in the doorway wearing her wedding dress. A nervous Prince Patrick was trembling at her side.

'This . . . this monstrosity is supposed to be my pony?' Petronella fumed. 'It looks like last year's unwanted Christmas tree!'

'Please, Your Almost Royalness. Truly, underneath it all, Sparkle's lovely,' Olivia pleaded, 'and she wants more than anything to be your wedding pony.'

'It's true, princess, babes!' Sparkle said. 'I do, I do.'

Petronella snorted. 'Me? On top of that beastly

glitter dingbat? It would ruin MY SPECIAL DAY!'

'Uhhh,' Prince Patrick piped up, 'isn't it actually *our* wedding day, my beloved? I'm not being pushy but I just wonder if you're being a little harsh and—'

'Oh, shut up, Patrick!' Petronella barked. 'Make yourself useful and grab my train before it gets muddy! I've had enough of this. I'm leaving!'

'Petronella, please,' Eliza begged. 'I know this looks bad but it's all Horace's fault and if Sparkle doesn't take part in the royal wedding then she'll never be free of the curse and the ponies will stay spellbound for all eternity!'

'Ha!' Petronella laughed. 'Whatever spell your pony is under is none of my affair! Let them stay cursed, I say!'

Now sitting at the back of the stables on a hay bale, Horace gave a particularly nasty chortle at this. 'Oooh, princess-to-be, not even a wicked queen could be so mean!' He clapped his chubby hands in glee. 'I really do like you!'

Petronella glared at him and gave a haughty flick of her long blonde hair before she returned her attention to Sparkle. 'As for you,' she sniped, 'you stupid, whinnying mud heap, you are absolutely, positively off my wedding list – FOREVER!'

And, with Prince Patrick scurrying behind clutching her train, Lady Petronella stormed out. In her wake the haunting wicked laughter of Horace the Hunt Master filled the air along with the disco smoke, ringing until the last vapours were gone.

Chapter Five

There was silence in the stables and then a whimpering, and soon the sounds of great heaving sobs filled the entire stables. The sobs were coming from the mud heap.

'Sparkle?' Olivia said. 'Oooh no! Please don't cry!'

'Boohoo-hoo!' Sparkle began to wail. 'Oh, Livvy and Eliza! All Sparkle ever wanted was to walk the bride down the aisle on a happy wedding day!'

And now I've gone and ruined everything!'

'Poor, poor pony!' Olivia raced to her side to comfort her, but through the mud and glitter she couldn't tell which bit of Sparkle she was supposed to pat. She took a guess and placed her hand gently on what she hoped was her neck. 'There, there. You mustn't blame yourself. It was that awful Horace.'

'He's very tricky,' Eliza agreed, 'but if Sparkle remains trapped by the witch's curse forever, what about the other ponies? We have to save them one by one – and if Sparkle stays stuck then surely the curse remains and the others will be stuck too?'

Sparkle sobbed even harder. 'Oh no! You mean all the other poor ponies will never be free because of me?'

Olivia was gobsmacked. 'Eliza! Now look what you've done!'

'Oops,' Eliza said. 'I'm so sorry! I really didn't mean to upset you, Sparkle. Please stop crying!'

But Sparkle couldn't stop crying. She was wailing like mad and, with each sob, massive hot tears ran down her face. As they coursed down her muzzle they created a miniature mudslide and the gunk and the glitter began to wash away.

'Boohoo-hoo!' Sparkle's tears had become a fountain and Olivia began to see streaks of snow-white fur beneath the caked-on mud and glitter.

'Please stop crying, Sparkle!' Eliza said.

'No!' Olivia shrieked. 'Don't stop crying! Keep crying!'

'What?' Sparkle croaked. 'You want me to cry? Livvy, babes, that's a bit mean!'

'I'm not being mean!' Olivia raced into Sparkle's stall and came back with a mirror. She showed the weeping pony her reflection. 'Look, Sparkle! Underneath the mud, where the tears have been, I can see *you*!'

Sparkle looked in the mirror. 'Oh, I see!' she exclaimed. 'Yes! That's me! That's how I used to be!'

Olivia dashed away again and this time came back with a halter. Her eyes were shining with excitement. 'Sparkle! I think we can fix it. You're going to be in that wedding after all!'

'I am?' Sparkle sniffled. 'Really and truly? You're not just saying that to stop me being sad?'

'Really and truly,' Olivia said. 'Don't you see, Sparkle? Beneath all that mud you look totally different. You're a stunning pure-white pony.'

'Ooooh!' Eliza was getting the idea too. 'So if we were to take all the mud off and get you clean, then the princess-to-be wouldn't even recognise you!'

'That's right!' agreed Olivia. 'She would think you were a different pony entirely.'

'So she could still choose me!' Sparkle had grasped the plan too. 'But, babes, Sparkle can't keep on crying forever!' she said. 'There's not enough tears inside to get all this mud and glitter off me!'

'We don't have to use tears,' Olivia said. 'We could

use soap and water as well.' Olivia paused to let her words sink in.

'Soap and water?' Sparkle began to tremble. 'You mean . . . a bath?'

'That's right,' Olivia confirmed.

Sparkle looked terrified and Olivia was tempted to hold on to the halter in case she tried to bolt, but she knew it was no use. She could never hold a Spellbound pony against its will.

'It's up to you, Sparkle. Will you do it?'

Sparkle gave a high-pitched whinny followed by a very determined neigh. 'Livvy, babes! Take me to the wash bay! This is going to be the day Sparkle comes clean!'

In the wash bay Olivia rolled up her sleeves, stuck on her wellies and began to hose. And hose. And hose.

'The mud and the glitter are so gooey and thick!' Olivia grumbled as she scrubbed hard with her sponges.

'But look! It's working!' Eliza said cheerfully from the side. 'I'd love to help you, of course, but . . .' She reached for a sponge and her fingers went straight through it as if it were made of mist!

'It's okay,' Olivia said to her best friend. 'I know you'd help if you could. It's not your fault that ghosts can't touch stuff and—'

'Oh!' Eliza gasped. 'Oh, Livvy! I can see her! I can see Sparkle!'

The mud had slid off in great chunks like an avalanche on a mountain slope, and beneath all the grime and grit there indeed was Sparkle – her gleaming white coat as pure as winter snow.

'Sparkle!' Olivia was excited now too. 'Oooh yes!'

'Keep going, babes!' Sparkle trilled. 'I'm feeling more like myself every minute!'

Olivia worked tirelessly, scrubbing until her arms were sore, and then hosing again until at last the mud heap was entirely gone and in its place stood a stunning white pony.

Olivia stood back with Eliza to assess her hard work. 'Oh my sweet potatoes!'

Sparkle gave her silky mane a shake and she swished her stark white tail. 'Do I look all right then, babes?' she asked anxiously. 'I feel naked. I've been caked under all that mud for a long time.'

'Sparkle,' Olivia said, 'I think you need to see for yourself.'

Olivia lugged the mirror all the way to the wash bay and propped it up against the wall.

Sparkle was shaking. She had her eyes shut tight. 'Oooh, I can't look! I'm scared.'

'Don't be afraid,' Olivia said soothingly. 'Open your eyes, Sparkle, and trust me.'

Sparkle opened her eyes.

'You see?' Olivia breathed. 'Sparkle, you are the most beautiful pony I have ever seen.'

It was true. Sparkle was stunning. Her coat, which was exactly the same shade of white as a wedding gown, was glossy and pure. Her mane, which flowed down over her shoulders, was silken like spun silver. Her tail trailed out behind her like a bridal veil.

'Oh, babes!' Sparkle said. And she burst into tears.

'Sparkle's crying again!' Eliza was shocked.

'Yes –' Olivia beamed – 'but this time they're tears of joy.'

'Oh, it's true, babes! Boohoo, boohoo!' Sparkle wept. 'Oh, Livvy and Eliza, you've made me the happiest pony in the world.'

Olivia was realising just how exhausting washing a pony could be. 'I think that will do for today, Sparkle,' she said, collapsing . 'I'm so tired, and it seems like most of the mud from you has somehow ended up on me!

'The next bit will be the fun part!' Eliza said, grinning. 'And I can help. I'm an expert on plaiting and primping. We need to pull out every trick we've got to make Sparkle look truly amazing so the princess-to-be will choose her for the royal procession.'

'We must give her the WOW factor,' Olivia agreed.

'Be here bright and early in the morning,' Eliza said, waving goodbye.

'Ta-ra, babes!' Sparkle cooed.

As Olivia walked down the lane, weary to the bone, she was certain tomorrow would be a triumph.

Chapter Six

Olivia bounded into the house without bothering to take off her mud-covered wellies. She stomped through the kitchen spreading dirty footprints. Her mum was nowhere to be seen.

'Whew!' Olivia sighed. 'I really couldn't cope with being told off right now!'

She opened her bedroom door.

'Hello, Livvy.'

Mrs Campbell was standing in the middle

of the messy room.

'You and I need to have a little talk.'

It was not a 'little talk' as it turned out. It was a very long rant.

'I've had enough, Olivia!' Mrs Campbell fumed. And Olivia knew it was serious because her mum had used her full name, which she only did when she was really cross. 'I've asked you a million times to clean your bedroom and you keep wiggling out of it. And speaking of wiggling out of things – I went to move the pizza box you'd left on the floor and there is a family of mice living in it!'

'I'm going to clean it!' Olivia objected. 'Honest!'

'Then get cracking!' Mrs Campbell said. 'Right now!'

'Now?' Olivia groaned. 'Mum! I'm exhausted!'

'Exhausted? From what?' Mrs Campbell

narrowed her eyes and Olivia realised she had no excuse. She couldn't tell her mum that she'd just spent the entire morning washing a magical pony with her best friend, a two-hundred-year-old ghost. There was nothing else for it. She took off her wellies and rolled up her sleeves again. It was time to clean.

For the rest of the afternoon Olivia sorted her way through the piles of clothes on her floor. But by dinner time she still couldn't see the carpet.

'You've been at it a while. How's it going in there?' her mum asked as she served up schnitzel and mashed potatoes.

'There's too much to do!' Olivia moaned. 'I'll never get it done in time.'

'You know,' Mrs Campbell said, 'if you kept your room tidy in the first place, you wouldn't be in this pickle.'

'I hear there was a family of mice living a pizza

box,' Ella said smugly. 'I keep my bedroom tidy. There are no hidden secrets in my room.'

Olivia put down her knife and fork in shock. 'That's it!' she said. 'There *is* a hidden secret in my bedroom!'

Mrs Campbell groaned. 'Not more mice!'

Olivia gobbled the rest of her dinner and returned to her room in great excitement. In all the mess she had created she had totally lost track of her things, and she kept unearthing treasures. But there was one secret treasure that still remained hidden. It was a golden box and she hadn't laid eyes on it since her eighth birthday.

'But it has to be here somewhere,' Olivia said. 'It has to be!'

Yet as she sorted her toys and folded her clothes she began to give up hope.

It was after midnight, when Olivia was stacking

away a pile of jumpers, that beneath them she saw
. . . the golden box!

'Please let it still be in here . . .' she breathed.

She opened the box and clapped her hands with
glee. 'Oh yay! It's all here! Oh yes! This is definitely
going to help Sparkle win!'

Olivia closed the box again and locked it to keep it safe. Then she gazed with satisfaction around her now perfectly tidy room, and finally, exhausted by the day's events, she tucked herself up in bed with the box held tight to her chest for safekeeping and fell asleep.

'Well! I don't believe it!' Mrs Campbell looked around the bedroom approvingly. She had checked under the bed. She'd even looked in the wardrobe. It was true – Olivia's bedroom really was tidy.

'You've done an amazing job, Livvy! Your room looks the best it ever has!'

'So can I go to the stables now?' Olivia already had the golden box tucked under her arm.

'I don't see why not,' Mrs Campbell said. 'Just make sure to be back by—'

But Olivia had already gone.

Eliza was relieved to see her. 'Livvy! Quick – we need to start. I've just heard that there's an inspection of prospective ponies today at midday at the royal palace. We have to get Sparkle all plaited up and we don't have much time.' She looked at the box under Olivia's arm. 'What's that?'

'This box,' said Olivia, 'is our secret weapon. You remember yesterday you said we needed something special to make Sparkle stand out from the other ponies? Well, I've found it. Look inside.' She opened the box for her.

'Diamonds and pearls!' Eliza cooed. 'Is it pirate treasure?'

'It's better than that,' Olivia said. 'It's a makeover kit.' She tipped the contents of the box on to the stable straw. 'There are glittery hairclips and shiny hair ribbons, pretty bows and diamante scrunchies,' she said, sorting through the items. 'I thought we could use them all in Sparkle's mane and tail.'

'Oooh yes!' Eliza agreed. 'This is exactly what I was talking about. With these jewels glittering against her white coat Sparkle will look perfect for a bride to ride.'

'Ooooh, babes!'

It was Sparkle. She was standing in her stall and eyeing up the jewelled hairclips and bows that Eliza and Olivia had just brought in, which were now scattered across the floor.

'Sparkle loves to accessorise!' she cried. 'Oh, Livvy, make me over, babes! The other ponies will be well jel when they see this!'

'I'm going to need help from Eliza this time,' Olivia said. 'I don't know how to plait a pony's mane.'

Eliza smiled. 'We'll do it together. You'll be my hands and I'll guide you.'

And that was how they worked, Eliza explaining to Livvy how to section and divide the mane and braid it into tiny plaits and roll them into neat, tight rosettes. The hairclips secured each rosette with a diamond and pearl.

'And for the tail,' Olivia said, 'we'll need lots of white ribbons for the plait and then we can scatter

crystals all through the strands so that Sparkle shimmers when she swishes it back and forth.'

'Ooh, please hurry, babes!' Sparkle snorted. 'It's almost midday. Sparkle needs to get to the palace on time!'

'Done!' Olivia cried at last. 'That's the last crystal! Is everything okay?'

'There's no time to check it!' Eliza cried. 'We need to go.'

The stall had filled with enchanted mist that was so dense it cloaked them all. When at last it cleared the girls and Sparkle were on the lawn of the royal palace and trumpets were blowing like mad.

A courtier was making an announcement. 'All ponies line up! Her Royal Almostness the princess-to-be Petronella is about to arrive!'

There was nothing more Olivia could do. It was all up to Sparkle now. It was choosing time.

Chapter Seven

On to the front lawn of the palace the ponies trotted forth.

'They all look so beautiful!' Sparkle groaned. 'Oh, Livvy, Eliza, do you really think Lady Petronella will choose me?'

'Of course she will, Sparkle,' Livvy said, trying to boost the pony's confidence. In her heart, though, Olivia was worried too. She hadn't expected such fierce competition.

'They're all such astonishing colours!' she whispered to Eliza. 'Look! There's a pink pony with white socks, and a golden one with a crimson blaze.'

More colours came strutting out on to the lawn. A violet mare with a flaxen mane and tail and a dapple-blue pony with dark eyes and sooty socks.

'Crikey!' Olivia boggled. 'I didn't know ponies came in rainbow colours!'

'They don't!' Eliza said. 'I think they've had these colours painted on. I just wonder who could have done this . . .'

As she said this a hunting horn sounded and across the fields a rabble of unruly hounds came bounding. The hounds ducked and dived and

scattered among the ponies, slobbering and baying as they raced across the palace lawn.

Following behind, riding on his horse, came the rotund red-coated figure of Horace the Hunt Master.

'What's he doing here?' Olivia asked. 'And what's that weird thing he's carrying? It looks a bit like a cannon!'

'It's a short, fat toy gun!' Eliza said. 'What do you suppose he's going to do?

'Oh no!' Olivia said. 'Eliza, I think the painted ponies are all Horace's doing!' She looked at the line-up. 'And the only pony who isn't painted yet is Sparkle.'

Horace had halted his horse now and had set about stuffing a bright green paint bomb into the gun.

'Prepare to meet your painter, Sparkle!' Horace chortled.

'He's going to turn me green!?' Sparkle shrieked.

'But I look terrible in green! It's not my colour at all. I'll never get chosen for the wedding if I look like a leprechaun!'

Sparkle began dashing back and forth, weaving in between the other ponies.

'Stand still!' Horace demanded. 'Stop or I'll . . . I'll shoot!'

'Keep running, Sparkle!' Olivia and Eliza shouted. 'He can't use his gun if he can't find his target!'

'Huff . . . puff . . . Sparkle can't keep this up . . .' Sparkle panted. 'Sparkle's getting tired, babes . . .'

'She's slowing down,' Eliza squeaked. 'Oh no! And now Horace is taking aim!'

Horace had Sparkle in his sights. The gun was loaded. He pointed the barrel at her and pulled the trigger.

'Sparkle! Noooooooo . . .!'

Olivia saw the paint ball fire out of the throat of the gun and Sparkle shut her eyes, ready to take the blow. But it never came. For at that very moment Olivia threw herself in front of the pony, taking the paint ball like a hero as it struck her squarely in her chest.

'Oof!' Olivia collapsed on the ground in a shower of green slime.

'Livvy!' Eliza shrieked and ran to her side. 'Oh no! You've turned invisible!'

'No I haven't,' Olivia replied. 'I'm just the same colour as the lawn, that's all.'

'Oh yes!' Eliza was relieved. 'There you are! I see you now!'

Olivia sat up. 'Where's Sparkle? Is she okay?'

'She escaped without a splash of paint!' Eliza said. 'And just in time because the princess-to-be has arrived.'

Tan-ta-ta-rah! Once again the trumpets were blaring as Lady Petronella stepped forth to begin her inspection.

'Ooooh, I can't look!' Eliza whispered as Lady Petronella marched up and down the line, examining each pony in turn. Finally she stopped.

'The pink pony!' Lady Petronella said. And Olivia's heart fell until she added, 'The pink pony . . . is very pretty . . . but not at all the sort of colour I'd choose for my wedding. No! Dismiss the pink pony!

In her place bring forth the golden pony and the dapple blue!'

Olivia's heart was racing like mad.

'The golden one is the same colour as my beautiful blonde hair,' Lady Petronella said, holding up a mirror to admire her own hair, 'and the dapple-blue one would match my eyes . . . and yet . . . no. They aren't quite right . . .'

Lady Petronella went back to the row of ponies and this time her hand touched Sparkle's muzzle.

'A white pony in the exact same shade as my wedding gown! And look at the diamonds and pearls woven into the plaits on her spotless mane and the way the crystals shimmer like stars in her tail!'

Lady Petronella turned to her footman. 'I choose the white one!' she said. 'Dismiss the rest. Have this pony taken into the palace and fitted in royal wedding finery. I shall ride her tomorrow in full

bridal regalia for my SPECIAL DAY. Ummm, I mean
. . . when I marry Prince Patrick.'

'Yes, Your Almost Highness.' The footman bowed
and stepped up to take Sparkle by the reins.

'Yaasss, queen!' Sparkle hooted as they led her off
towards the palace. 'I'm the chosen one! Don't wait
up for me, Eliza and Livvy, babes. It's a party at
the palace and I'll be home late!'

'There she goes!' Eliza trilled. 'Sparkle the royal
wedding pony. Oh, Livvy, we did it! We've beaten the
curse of Spellbound Stables once more!'

'Hmmm, but did we?' Olivia said.

Eliza frowned. 'What do you mean?'

'Well, usually when we help a pony to mend its
ways, then the moment the curse is broken there's a
sudden blinding flash of golden light and, hey presto,
they become a real-life pony again!'

'Why yes, that is what usually occurs,' Eliza agreed.

'So why didn't it happen this time?' Olivia was confused.

'Oh, I expect it's just a formality,' Eliza said breezily. 'Spells are a very exact business and since Sparkle's transformation is all about her wish to be a wedding pony I'm certain the spell will break when her wish comes true on the wedding day. You'll see.'

'I hope so,' Olivia said. 'All the same, I feel strangely anxious.'

'Oh, don't be!' Eliza said. 'Livvy, you worry too much. It's all going perfectly to plan. Nothing can stop us now. You heard Lady Petronella. Tomorrow when the wedding bells ring at last Sparkle's curse will truly be broken forever.'

Chapter Eight

It was the morning of the royal wedding. Olivia, who was now in possession of a very tidy bedroom, searched through her highly organised wardrobe, quickly found her jodhpurs and set off for the stables.

'Sparkle, are you ready to go?' she called out as she stepped into the Spellbound pony's stall.

'Close your eyes!' It was Eliza.

'Why?'

'It's a surprise,' Eliza said.

Olivia reluctantly shut her eyes. 'Okay.'

There was giggling and clomping about in the corridor.

'You can open them now,' Eliza trilled.

Olivia opened her eyes. 'Wowsers!' she cried.

Sparkle was standing in front of her and Olivia had never seen anything like it in her life. The pony was dressed with a tutu round her waist in thick frilly layers of snow-white tulle trimmed with gold. She wore gold booties on her hooves and her saddle was flounced with the plumes of white ostrich feathers that stuck out at the sides, giving the impression that she had wings. On her head were more plumes and attached to her bridle was a golden tiara hung with tulle that covered Sparkle's muzzle.

'It's a *bridle* veil,' Eliza pointed out.

Olivia rolled her eyes. 'Very punny!'

'Well, babes?' Sparkle said anxiously. 'Tell Sparkle the truth! Is it a bit much?'

'Sparkle,' Olivia said with a smile, 'you look AMAZEY-MAZEY WEDDING DAZEY!'

Sparkle whinnied and kicked up her hooves in delight. She squealed with joy. 'Oooh, I do, don't I? Sparkle knew you'd love it! Oh, come on. Let's go, Livvy, babes! It's time! The wedding is about to begin!'

The two girls stepped into Sparkle's stall and as the enchanted mist rose up around their ankles Sparkle began to hum. 'Dum-dum-de-dum!' she warbled. 'Here comes the bride, taking me for a ride . . .'

And suddenly it wasn't just Sparkle who was singing the tune. A string quartet was playing the wedding march. They had arrived.

'Crikey!' Olivia breathed. 'This is unbelievable!'

They were inside the royal palace in what Olivia assumed must be the grand ballroom and everywhere you looked the place was in chaos.

'Quick! More roses! More lilies!' the florist was shouting.

'More Chantilly cream! More vanilla sponge for the butterfly cake wings!' the cake maker was crying.

'Put more puff in those sleeves,' the dressmaker was pleading with the seamstress. 'And hurry up ... she's coming ... she's coming!'

'Too late!' the seamstress yelped. 'She's here!'

Into the room stormed Lady Petronella. She was so furious the air seemed to tremble around her as she thundered through the grand ballroom.

'Footmen!' she screamed. 'Why am I on the grubby floor? Where is the red carpet that should be flung out in front of me to cushion my toesies?'

The footmen scurried forward to roll out the red carpet in her path and while they were still straightening the edges Lady Petronella stomped onwards, crushing the footmen's hands beneath her heels as she walked over them.

'Oww, owww, owww!' the footmen said, wincing.

'Oh, shut up, you big babies!' Lady Petronella snapped at them. 'And you!' She turned on the florist. 'Who told you to use lilies? Vulgar flowers! They're not fit for an almost-princess like me!'

Lady Petronella stomped past the butterfly cakes and without pausing she began to pull the wings off all the butterflies. 'Awful!' she shrieked. 'I despise Chantilly cream!'

The dressmaker was cowering as Petronella pulled on the wedding dress and stepped out of the dressing room to stare in the mirror. 'Ugh. Still. Not. Puffy. Enough!' Lady Petronella tugged cruelly at her sleeves. 'I hate it. It's utterly hideous – but it's too late, so I suppose it will have to do!'

The dressmaker gave a quiet heart-wrenching sob. 'My beautiful dress! It took six months to make it!'

'Oh, who cares, crybaby?' Lady Petronella laughed. 'You're all crybabies, the lot of you.' She was still stomping along the red carpet and now she had reached Sparkle.

'And you!' She scowled at the pony. 'Look at your wings and crown! You're far too fabulous by far! You're going to get all the attention and everyone will be looking at you when they should be staring at me, me, ME! This is *my* SPECIAL DAY and nobody should ever forget it!'

In a frenzy Lady Petronella grabbed Sparkle's ostrich-feather wings and plucked them off! Then she tore off the tutu and yanked off Sparkle's tiara and threw it away.

Sparkle's bottom lip quivered and she looked as if she were about to burst into tears but she said nothing as Lady Petronella flung the costume aside and turned back to survey what she had done.

'There!' she said. 'Now you're a very plain, boring pony, which means that everyone will be looking only at me – which is just as it should be on my SPECIAL DAY! Oh! Wait a minute! There are still diamonds in your tail. That will never do . . .'

'Excuse me? Your Almost Highness?' The head footman had suddenly appeared at her side. 'I hate to interrupt but we do need to leave. Prince Patrick is already at the cathedral and he's waiting for you to arrive so you can marry him.'

Lady Petronella groaned. 'Yes, yes, I'm coming.'

She fluffed about with her gown and then glared at him. 'Well? What are you waiting for? Help me up on to my pony! That's your job, isn't it?'

There was much grunting and shoving as the footman pushed Lady Petronella in her enormous meringue of a wedding dress up, up, up until at last she was on Sparkle's back.

'Whew! It really is a very puffy dress!' Lady Petronella exclaimed. Then she cast her cruel eyes around the palace. 'Where are my trumpeters? I can't leave without fanfare!'

'Here we are, Your Almost Highness!'

The trumpeters ran to her side and began to play and Sparkle pranced through the halls of the grand palace past Olivia and Eliza who had been watching the whole commotion in disbelief.

'This is it, babes!' Sparkle cried as she trotted by. 'Wish me luck, Eliza and Livvy! It's wedding time!'

Chapter Nine

The roar of the crowd was deafening as Lady Petronella and Sparkle emerged on to the streets.

'Hooray for Almost-Princess Petronella!' A little girl ran forward to throw a handful of confetti.

'Dreadful child! Stop flinging stuff at me!' Lady Petronella shrieked in reply.

'It's confetti, Lady Pet, babes!' Sparkle said. 'She's celebrating! They all are! Everybody loves a wedding.'

'Do they?' Lady Petronella sniffed haughtily. 'I suppose for these commoners it must be marvellous to see me in all my splendour on my SPECIAL DAY. All the same, if that child throws anything at me again, I shall have her put in the dungeons.'

Lady Petronella gave Sparkle a sharp dig with her heels. 'Come on, useless pony. This is boring me! Hurry to the cathedral!'

'Oooh, Lady Pet, babes!' said Sparkle. 'Your wish is my command! Sparkle's on the trot!'

Outside the cathedral, Olivia and Eliza, who had run on ahead, found Prince Patrick.

'Sparkle and Lady Petronella are on their way!' Olivia told him. 'They'll be arriving any moment.'

'Ah, so they're almost here then?' Prince Patrick looked anxious. 'Tell me, is the Lady Petronella in a good mood, do you think? Only this morning she was very grumpy indeed. She threw two footmen in the dungeon before we'd even had breakfast.'

'She's been a teensy bit grouchy,' Eliza admitted.

'More than a teensy bit,' Olivia said. 'She's, well ... she's gone fully bridal bonkers.'

'Bridal bonkers?' Prince Patrick looked even more nervous.

'I'm afraid so,' Olivia said. 'She's been shouting at everyone.'

'The florist,' said Eliza, 'and the poor cake maker!'

'And the dressmaker,' added Olivia. 'And Sparkle.'

'Oh dear,' Prince Patrick said. 'She's really not very nice at the best of times and a wedding has brought out the worst in her.'

'I wonder, Patrick,' Olivia said kindly, 'if perhaps Lady Petronella isn't the right girl for you to marry after all ...'

'I wonder too,' Prince Patrick admitted.
'Except it's a bit late now . . .'

'Because here they come!' Eliza said. 'Oh, doesn't
Sparkle look like a fairy tale?'

'She's so clean and shiny!' Olivia agreed. 'And,
uhhh, Lady Petronella looks very determined and a
little cross.'

'Yikes!' said Prince Patrick. 'She's probably
furious that we're out here milling about! We'd
better get up the aisle and be ready for her to make
her grand entrance.'

The three of them scurried hastily inside and the
girls found a spot in a pew right at the front while
Prince Patrick went to stand with the bishop. They
had only just got into position when the string quartet
swelled into song and the wedding march began.

Lady Petronella and Sparkle made their
grand entrance.

'Here comes the bride! Here comes the bride!'
Sparkle hummed merrily as she trotted up the aisle.

'Quiet, you ridiculous pony!' snapped Lady
Petronella. 'You're ruining my SPECIAL DAY with
your nonsense.'

101

Sparkle fell silent and as the music ended the pony came to a halt to allow Lady Petronella to slide off her back to take her place in front of the bishop and by Prince Patrick.

'Uhhh . . . you look lovely, darling!' Prince Patrick whispered.

'Well, duh!' Lady Petronella snapped at him. Then she straightened her frock, shoved her posy of flowers at Sparkle to hang on to and glared hard at the bishop. 'Well? What are you waiting for standing there in your silly pointy hat? Marry us!'

The bishop looked very nervous and cleared his throat. 'Dearly beloved, we are gathered here today—'

'Oh yes, yes, yes. BORING! Get on with it and marry us now or I'll have you thrown in the dungeons!' Lady Petronella barked.

The bishop cleared his throat and cut to the

chase. 'If there is anyone here who has any reason why Patrick and Petronella should not be joined in marriage, let them speak now . . .'

'I do!'

There was a gasp from the crowd.

'Who said that?' the bishop asked.

The eyes of the whole cathedral were upon her as Sparkle put her hoof up.

'Me, Bishop, babes. I said it.'

'The pony?' The bishop was baffled. 'But why do you want to stop the wedding?'

'I don't want to be unkind, babes,' Sparkle said, snorting, 'but we've all noticed how Lady Petronella's dead mean and poor Prince Patrick, well, he's lovely, ain't he? It just doesn't seem fair that he should get lumbered with her.'

'Of all the insults!' Lady Petronella hissed. 'And on my SPECIAL DAY! Sparkle, you're going be sent to the dungeons the minute this wedding is done!'

Lady Petronella turned to the bishop. 'Don't listen to the pony! Finish it!' she shouted. 'Go ahead and make us married – now!'

The bishop looked terrified. 'Uhh . . . by the power vested in me I now pronounce you man and wife. Prince Patrick, you may kiss the bride!'

'But I don't want to . . .' Prince Patrick began to resist but before he could object any more Lady Petronella lunged at him with her lips puckered up!

'Oh no!' Eliza cried out. 'Once she kisses him they'll be married forever!'

'Somebody stop her!' Olivia shouted.

'Sparkle's on the trot, princey, babes!'

With a defiant shake of her mane Sparkle jumped between the bride and groom, and with a firm swish of her tail she knocked Lady Petronella aside.

Lady Petronella gave a shriek as she landed on

top of the bishop, and meanwhile Prince Patrick, who had been all puckered up bracing himself reluctantly to take the kiss, found himself somehow smacking his lips square on Sparkle's cheek!

'Oh my!' Sparkle blushed. 'Oooh, Prince Patrick, you kissed me! Oooh, I shall never wash my cheek again! All the other ponies are going to be well jel when I tell . . . Oooh, goodness! What's happening?

I'm feeling all funny and tickly inside! Oooh, Livvy, Eliza! Help me! What's going on?'

'Look!' Olivia said. 'Sparkle's glowing!'

The pony was bathed in the most amazing golden light. It beamed and shone with such power that it filled the cathedral.

'Oooh, Livvy, babes!' Sparkle rose on her hind legs as the golden light grew brighter. 'The light is so magical, it's making Sparkle feel all . . .'

But Sparkle never did get to say how she felt because at that moment the pony stopped talking and began neighing instead.

'The Pemberley Witch's spell has been broken!' Eliza squeaked.

'Oh hooray!' Olivia cried. 'Sparkle's a real-life pony again; she's free!'

Sparkle seemed to realise it too because the pony

began whinnying with delight as Eliza and Olivia jumped for joy.

Prince Patrick, however, looked rather confused. 'Did I do that?' he asked Eliza. 'I've heard that a prince's kiss is very powerful magic. Is that what transformed her?'

Eliza was about to explain to him about the witch's curse but then she saw Olivia giving her a cheeky look.

'Ummmm, I mean, possibly it could be your kiss that did it,' she said. 'You know, they do say true love's kiss can do that.'

'I wouldn't smooch any frogs if I were you,' Olivia added with a wink, 'just to be on the safe side.'

'Right,' Prince Patrick said. 'Good advice, Livvy. I shall heed it.'

'What about me?' Lady Petronella huffed as she clambered back to her feet. 'Isn't anyone going to even ask if I'm okay? That awful pony knocked me over and ruined my SPECIAL DAY!'

'I rather think you ruined your own day, Lady Petronella,' Prince Patrick said, giving Sparkle a pat on the neck. 'The pony was quite right – you're far too mean for me. The wedding is off!'

'Hooray for Prince Patrick!' cried the florist and the cake maker who were sitting in the front pew enjoying the spectacle.

'And for Sparkle too!' called the dressmaker with a hoot.

And suddenly the cathedral was going wild with applause as Lady Petronella stomped out in a huff and Prince Patrick, Eliza and Olivia made their way up the aisle with Sparkle dancing gaily beside them, whinnying with joy in a shower of confetti and sunshine.

Chapter Ten

It seemed a shame to let the wedding feast go to waste and so a picnic was held that afternoon at Spellbound Stables.

'These egg-and-cress club sandwiches are just brilliant – you must have one!' Patrick told Olivia, passing her the plate. 'I say, Eliza, if you've had enough to eat, do you think you'd fancy a sword fight? It's been quite a day and often I find the best thing to do at the end of a busy day is have a sword fight. How about it? Shall we duel?'

'Oooh, yes please!' Eliza beamed. 'Wait here! I'll get my sword . . .'

And so, while the two of them raced up and down the corridor and bounded over walls as they clashed blades, Olivia practiced braiding Sparkle's mane.

'Oh rats!' she complained. 'I managed to do a perfect braid and then Sparkle shook her head and it's all fallen apart. I'll have to start again.'

Sparkle shook her mane yet again and Eliza laughed. 'Oooh, Livvy, babes, I think Sparkle is tired of being fussed over and wants to go and play with the other ponies,' Eliza said.

And so Olivia let Sparkle loose in the field with Bess and Prince and the three ponies galloped and reared and ran about wildly with glee. Then the girls and Prince Patrick went back inside the stables to Sparkle's old stall where their dessert, a very big cake with white icing, was waiting for them.

'This is extremely yummy!' Eliza had helped herself to a large slice and started scoffing it.

'Wait . . .' Olivia asked suspiciously. 'Patrick? Is this wedding cake?'

'Umpfhl,' Prince Patrick tried to answer but his mouth was full. 'Well, yes, it seemed a shame to let it go to waste!'

'Hooray!' Eliza said, helping herself to a second

piece. 'Here's to royal weddings!'

'And to the Spellbound ponies!' Olivia said. 'May they all soon be free!'

At that moment, a gust of ghostly mist swept through the stable doors, and there came the haunting bay of the hunting hounds.

'Oh no,' Olivia said, 'the dogs are here!'

'How many times do I have to tell you, Olivia?' An icy voice echoed through the corridor. 'They are not dogs. They are hounds, and you must always call them hounds, am I clear?'

Floating magically behind the hounds on a cloud of spooky mist, a very beautiful woman appeared. She wore a black silk top hat and a velvet riding coat. Her auburn hair fell in lush waves and her alabaster skin looked ghostly against her scarlet lips. One dark eyebrow arched in an imperious manner as she examined the scene in front of her.

'Who is this then?' she demanded.

Eliza broke the silence. 'Prince Patrick, I'd like you to meet my mother, Lady Luella of Pemberley Manor.'

'Oh, hullo!' Patrick bounded forward to shake her hand. 'Very nice to meet you, Mrs L. We were just eating the wedding cake. Would you like a piece?'

'I'm not here for cake!' Lady Luella arched her brows even higher. 'I'm here because I see you two girls have unbound yet another pony?'

'We have!' Olivia confirmed. 'And we're going to keep going until all the ponies are free – wait and see. And then Eliza will be unbound too and she and I will be real friends in a yard filled with wonderful ponies.'

Lady Luella's brows arched so high now they were almost through the roof and Olivia could have sworn something peculiar passed between mother and daughter as Lady Luella gave Eliza a very mysterious look.

'One more spell you've broken,' Lady Luella said as she hovered. 'The other spells remain. You'll need all your wits about you to break the chain. Farewell, Eliza, dear heart, until we meet again.'

And, in a puff of spectral smoke Lady Luella and the hounds were gone.

'I say,' Prince Patrick said, 'is it just me or is your mum a lot of fun, Eliza?'

Olivia sighed. 'It's just you.'

'Oh well.' Prince Patrick looked at his watch. 'It's been a long day. The king and queen will be expecting me home for supper, so I'd best be off.'

'Well, I'm going to have one more piece of cake ...' Eliza said, licking the icing off her fingers. 'And then Olivia and I had better press on too. We need to free the next Spellbound pony.'

'*Two brave girls*,' Olivia said.

'Together for ever,' Eliza agreed.

And, as they ate their cake and hatched their plans, back at the stables a new name was already beginning to materialise on the brass plaque on the door of the fourth stall. Another Spellbound pony would soon be here ...

NEXT IN THE SERIES . . .

Fortune and Cookies

Lady Luella of Pemberley Manor requests the company of her daughter, Eliza, and best friend, Olivia, for the 200th-year celebration fête. To be held on the manor lawn next Saturday at noon.

'What's a fête exactly?' said Olivia.

'It's like a big garden party and the whole village comes along,' Eliza explained. 'There are wonderful stalls selling treats of all kinds and animals on parade and lots of games—'

'Games? What kind of games?'

'Oh, the usual thing,' Eliza said. 'Guess the weight of the bull, duck racing, black-pudding hurling—'

'Duck racing? Wouldn't the jockeys have to be very, very small?'

Eliza laughed. 'Oh, now you're just being silly! No one rides them! But you can make a bundle betting on which of the ducks is the fastest. There'll be jugglers too, I imagine, and fire-eaters, and there's always a fortune-teller, and did I mention there's lots of scrummy food? Hot roasted chestnuts and sweet mince cakes . . .'

'It sounds like you want to go,' Olivia said.

'I suppose I do,' Eliza agreed. 'It's been two hundred years since the last one and I have so missed all the fun of the fair. There's always a big showjumping contest at the end. I actually won it myself once. I rode our Pemberley Golden Boy, Champ, Mama's boldest and most brilliant jumping pony, and we got a clear round even though the fences were frightfully huge!'

'Why do you think Lady Luella is holding the fête again after all this time?' Olivia was suspicious. 'You know she's always trying to get you to return home to live with her in the manor, Eliza.'

'Oh, she must know by now that I'll never leave Spellbound Stables until all the ponies are free,' Eliza said breezily. 'No, I expect it's just that she couldn't let the two hundredth anniversary go by without a celebration. Come on, Livvy, we should go. Did I mention there's lots of scrummy food?'

'I do like scrummy food . . .' Olivia admitted.

All this time, as the girls had been talking, the plaque on the stable door had been glowing more and more brightly, and now it shone and twinkled like a star.

Olivia gasped. 'Look! Do you see that? The name has appeared! It's time to summon a new pony!'

Eliza clapped her hands with glee. 'Time to cross the threshold!'

She stood beside Olivia and the two girls stepped into the stall and called out the name on the door. '*Champ!*' ...

To be continued ...

Out Now

hem all!